SUCCESS AT THE ACADEMY

A SECURITY DIRECTORATE SHORT STORY

ALEXANDRIA BLAELOCK

Also by Alexandria Blaelock

SHORT STORY COLLECTIONS
The Histories of Hayward Hall
Lovelorn, Lovestruck and Love at First Sight
Common or Garden Variety Heroes
Case Files of the Wilkinson Detective Agency
Unavoidable Fates
Christmas Travesties
Five Faces of Felicia Clarke
Little Place Called Home

FICTION
That Love Nonsense
Taipan vs Brown
The Ghost and Ms Cox
Friends Like That

MS BLAELOCK'S BOOKS
Stress Free Dinner Parties
Signature Wardrobe Planning
Holistic Personal Finance
Minimally Viable Housekeeping
Planning a Life Worth Living

A SELECTION OF AVAILABLE SHORT STORIES
Alma's Grace
Fate in Your Hands
Lady of the Looking Glass
Morning Star, Evening Star, Superstar
Secret Singer
Shining Star
Ship in a Bottle
Simone Says Hands in the Air
The Day the Schedule Broke

SUCCESS AT THE ACADEMY

A SECURITY DIRECTORATE SHORT STORY

ALEXANDRIA BLAELOCK

BlueMere Books

MELBOURNE, AUSTRALIA

For permission requests, please contact
enquiries@bluemerebooks.com.

Ordering Information:
Discounts are available on quantity purchases. For details, contact orders@bluemerebooks.com.

Success at the Academy/Alexandria Blaelock
paperback ISBN: 978-1-922744-76-0
digital ISBN: 978-1-922744-77-7

Book Layout © BookDesignTemplates.com
Cover Art © Tithi Luadthong/Depositphotos

SUCCESS AT THE ACADEMY

Number 124 was spiteful.

But in the dog-eat-dog world of the State Academy of Cultural Regulation, that was a good thing.

There's no point in a Eugenics Programme that doesn't produce the citizens you're looking for.

Lieutenant Jemima Hunt blew her whistle, generating a breath of mist in the cold gymnasium air, and gestured for the boy to stand aside.

He stood slightly bent over, panting from his exertions, then started pacing a little to ease the muscle ache.

His underpants and singlet were his only protection from the cold, and after a good ten minutes of running hard on the treadmill, there was no sign of the goosebumps he'd walked in with.

She was warm enough in her thick blue tactical uniform, with her tiny medals lined up precisely across her left breast.

The smell of the child's fear tasted like acid on her tongue.

Understandable.

Failing any of the physical tests disqualified the children from all.

And by now, he and the other children knew anyone who failed, disappeared from school with no explanation.

There one day, gone the next. Never seen again.

Pale grey daylight leaked through the deep-set windows set high in the thick walls, but the bright electric lights suspended on long wires from the ceiling revealed the half-starved boy in all his pathetic scrawniness.

Though he was less emaciated than some of his classmates.

In a school that trained you to stand out rather than fit in, he was doing okay.

This physical assessment marked the end of his first year of basic training. A pass guaranteed promotion to the second year and a uniform issue.

Hopefully, he'd preserve a cool head; some kids got too cocky and failed out of their second year.

The key to surviving long enough to graduate was a slow, sustained effort. Just enough to make an impression on the teachers, but not so much to make yourself a target for the other kids.

Pass your physical, psychological, medical, and academic examinations, but not too well.

The skills the kids were developing as they dealt with each other, the over and underachieving students, and ensuring conformity amongst themselves, gave them a good grounding for their future careers.

If they did not get severely injured, stayed alive and passed their exams, their rewards were names and a place in the Protection Squadron.

But if, like her, they manifested some kind of useful genetic ability, known colloquially as a "superpower," they'd earn a placement at the University of Civilisation for Officer Training.

Though you never discussed your powers.

And if they graduated University, a Security Directorate Bureau career that made the best use of their abilities.

The gym echoed with the sound of movement. Whistles peeped, and voices barked as instructors walked, stacked heels thudding across the wooden floor. Children grunted and gasped with effort as they ran and jumped through the tests.

Hunt heard a loud crack behind her, and a child's scream quickly choked off.

It wasn't her candidate, so she didn't turn to look.

But the boy could see what happened, and his pale face took on a greenish tinge. She watched him swallow and stand a little straighter.

Good.

If he failed this physical assessment, like the injured child, the Bureau would divert him to the Euthanasia Programme, and that would be the last anyone would see of him.

It was a mercy really. There were no places in the Security Directorate for people who couldn't hold their own. No one was permitted to drain resources dedicated to the greater good.

She took the time and distance measurements from the treadmill and noted them on his assessment sheet, along with comments on his reaction to the injured child.

Too soon to know where 124 would end up, or even if he would live to see the end of his second year of training.

But with fewer students, he'd have greater access to food and resources, and his odds would improve.

Especially if he worked hard to develop his physical strength enough to access supplies allocated to other students.

The early signs were good, so Hunt was pretty sure he'd get there. One way or another.

A gurney cleared the injured child away, the proceed signal sounded, and Hunt gestured for 124 to precede her to the next testing station.

"Push-ups," she barked, setting the metronome at five seconds and starting her stopwatch.

He dropped to the floor with a thud and started doing push-ups, keeping up with the metronome reasonably well to start, though it wasn't that long until he fell behind. Nicely average between the best and worse recorded results.

She blew the whistle, and he stood aside, flicking his arms and legs out to ease them while she wrote his results on the assessment.

While they waited for the signal to move ahead, she watched him, trying not to fidget excessively.

There was something familiar about him, but she couldn't quite place it.

The next test was flexibility, some quick stretches to see where he fit.

Following her instructions, he demonstrated his shoulder mobility by reaching one hand over his shoulder and the other behind his back to clasp his hands.

He made it look easy. She checked a box.

Then he sat, legs fully extended and bent to hold his toes.

Easy. Another check.

He lay face down on the floor, arms held out to his side, and lifted his chest from the ground.

A little harder, but another check.

They seemed like simple tests, but these numbers would benchmark his results for the rest of his schooling. The school expected him to improve them as the years went by.

At the next station, she crouched to observe how high he could jump from standing. Three jumps, 15 seconds apart - just enough time to note the distance between jumps.

Slightly higher than average, but this gave him room to manoeuvre as he bulked up on his way through puberty.

Next, the penultimate test; endurance. The one that had earlier seen the end of the screaming child.

Just a grab bar you had to jump to reach, pull your chin above, then hold on tightly for as long as possible.

As if your life depended on it. Which in a way it did, though the children didn't know that.

124 frowned and licked his lips as he approached.

His little anxious face reminded her of her younger brother.

In a moment of weakness, she took pity on him and gave him an extra few seconds to pull himself together before she blew the whistle and started the stopwatch.

The second hand seemed to tick in slow motion as the boy grimaced, arms quivering, trying to hold on.

Tick.

Tick.

Tick.

He groaned and let go, landing neatly on both feet.

Good. Reasonable time. Clean landing. No injury.

Hunt nodded as she noted the time on the assessment form.

He rotated his arms backwards and forwards, seeking to ease the ache.

Was it possible they were related?

Like all children who passed their Genomics Bureau postnatal testing, the hospital had removed him from his parents and placed him in the State Academy. Almost from birth, he'd undertaken intensive education and physical training.

Learned about the Security Directorate and his potential place within it, as a Guardian of the Public Good.

In a few years, as his indoctrination continued, he'd learn more about how the machinery worked, and the sacrifices they all made to keep the Directorate strong.

Given her "superpower", it was inevitable. Sooner or later, she'd meet a family member on their way through the Academy.

That was why stripped the children of their identity and raised them in anonymity; to remove the possibility of nepotism or other bias during training and assessments.

Though it also functioned to break the bonds of family ties.

Only a few of the founding families claimed their kin when the names and families when revealed. And most graduates realised they'd managed well enough without family connections, so saw no reason to start familial relationships.

By this stage, 124 had more or less passed his physical assessment.

Hunt handed him the dynamometer and adjusted his grip on the device. "Hold tight for five seconds," she said, blew the whistle and started the stopwatch.

She gave him a 15-second break as she noted the weight. Another try, and another break. The last attempt.

Reasonable effort, within the range expected.

Time to evaluate his body.

She waved a hand at the height gauge, and he stood beneath it. She adjusted the bar and took the measurement.

He moved to stand on the weight scales and she noted his weight.

After a quick calculation, she added his body mass index.

She gestured for him to approach her, and when he did, pulled his singlet up.

He flinched at the touch of her icy fingers, but didn't squirm or try to evade her.

She pinched a fold of skin from his abdomen, clipped it with callipers, and noted the body fat measurement on his assessment sheet.

Doing well.

Last step, body measurements to check his body development and tailor his new school uniform.

"Arms out."

She picked a tape measure up and checked his shoulder, chest, waist, arm and leg length and circumference.

As she wrote his measurements on the form, she snuck glances over her clipboard.

Of course, it was possible they were related.

She counted back to her prenatal confinement and looked at him again.

It was possible he was her son.

She hadn't taken his removal well.

The Genomics Bureau had extended her postnatal confinement while they monitored her condition. And increased her drug doses.

She'd felt his loss keenly, but that was just one of many sacrifices she'd made for the Greater Good.

If you wanted to live, you adapted and moved on.

She hadn't contested when her husband petitioned the Genomics Bureau to end their contract early.

She didn't blame him.

Given the events surrounding the birth, it was unlikely that she'd be paired with anyone else.

Unfortunate, but expected.

Hunt nodded her dismissal of 124 and pointed toward the exit door.

He bowed formally, turned smartly, and marched from the room.

Jemima clutched the clipboard to her chest and watched him leave before writing some notes on her general impressions of him, his attitude, and abilities.

She signed his sheet, passing his first physical examination of his basic training, granting him a promotion to second year.

Effectively authorising his continued existence.

Until the next assessment.

His life was about to get a lot more complicated than it already was. But at least it was a new life.

She looked up at the ceiling as she remembered the dormitory she'd grown up in. Bare concrete walls, cold concrete floors. A small steel bed frame next to a small steel locker.

The bare minimum of comforts to build strong characters.

Some kid from the country had smuggled a flower in and left in on her locker. She'd turned him in after she'd beaten him up.

Her single teacher's room was not so very different from the children's dormitories.

And these days she'd welcome a flower.

Even a dandelion.

Maybe it was time to apply to the Genomics Bureau and see what they had to offer.

It might be nice to be with someone.

To once again be someone's beloved.

THE END

ABOUT THE AUTHOR

Alexandria Blaelock writes stories, some of them for *Ellery Queen's Mystery Magazine* and *Pulphouse Fiction Magazine.*

She's also written five selfhelp books applying business techniques to personal matters like getting dressed, cleaning house, and feeding your friends.

She lives in a forest because she enjoys birdsong, and the smell of gum leaves. When not telecommuting to parallel universes from her Melbourne based imagination, she watches K-dramas, talks to animals, and drinks Campari. At the same time.
Discover more at www.alexandriablaelock.com.

IF YOU ENJOYED THIS STORY...

try the other Security Directorate stories

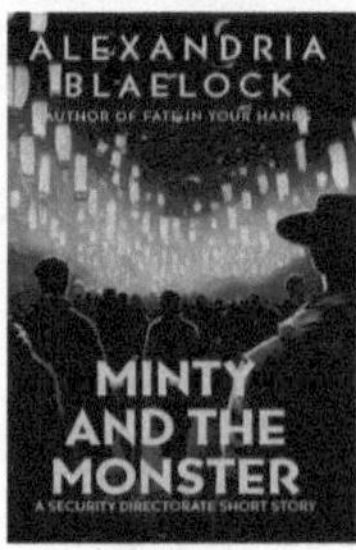

... or the collections

Why not try *The Ghost and Ms Cox*

Life interrupted

To say the letter was a surprise was an understatement. It arrived addressed to Miss Finlay Cox, which made the contents even more extraordinary.

Orphan Finn Cox inherits a cottage. Thinks it holds the key to her origins. Of course she takes a look. Who wouldn't?

But when she gets there, she gets more than she bargained for.

Is it friend, family or foe?

www.ingramcontent.com/pod-product-compliance
Lightning Source LLC
Chambersburg PA
CBHW030815190726

48285CB00003B/1191